A. J. P. TAYLOR

HOW
WARS
END

HAMISH HAMILTON
London

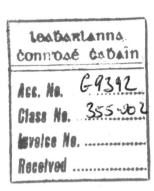
First published in Great Britain 1985
by Hamish Hamilton Ltd
Garden House 57-59 Long Acre London WC2E 9JZ

British Library Cataloguing in Publication Data
Taylor, A. J. P.
  How wars end.
  1. War   2. Pacific settlement of international
  disputes
  I. Title
  355'.028   U21.2
  ISBN 0-241-11458-6
  ISBN 0-241-11460-8 Pbk

Filmset by Pioneer
Printed and bound in Great Britain by
R. J. Acford Ltd, Chichester

HOW WARS END

CONTENTS

ILLUSTRATIONS

xi

LIST OF MAPS
(drawn by Patrick Leeson)

I

NAPOLEON'S
LAST GREAT WAR

Europe under Napoleon 1810

0	100	200	miles

100

100 300 km

Napoleonic Empire under Direct Rule

Dependent States under Napoleonic control

Allies of Napoleon before 1812

Route of Napoleon's advance
and retreat in Russia 1812

French defeat ✕ Waterloo (1815)

SCOTLAND

DENMARK

WALES

NORTH SEA

ENGLAND

London

KINGD'M OF
HOLLAND

W...
PHA...
CONF...
ERAT...
OF

Brussels
✕
Waterloo (1815)

Kaub

Rhine

R

✕ Laon (1814)

Paris (1814) ✕

✕ Rheims (1814)

✕ La Rothière (1814)

Fontainebleau

✕ La Fère
Champenoise (1814)

BADEN

ATLANTIC OCEAN

F
R
E
N
C
H

E
M
P
I
R

SWITZ.

KING
OF

PORTUGAL

S P A I N

Catalonia

CORSICA

Lisbon

• Madrid

KINGD'M OF
SARDINIA

St Petersburg

ESTHONIA

LIVONIA

S W E D E N

KURLAND

Dvina

BALTIC SEA

Vitebsk

Moscow

Borodino

× Maloyaroslavets
(1812)

Smolensk

Tilsit

Königsberg

Neman

Beresina

R U S S I A N

E M P I R E

P R U S S I A

in

GRAND DUCHY

Brest Litovsk

13)

XONY

Warsaw

OF WARSAW

Dnieper

GALICIA

A U S T R I A A U S T R O -

H U N G A R I A N

Dniester

Vienna

E M P I R E

BESSARABIA

M

H U N G A R Y

MOLDAVIA

Prut

LLYRÍAN

Trieste

PROVINCE

WALLACHIA

BLACK SEA

BOSNIA

SERBIA

Danube

ADRIATIC SEA

O T T O M A N

KINGD'M OF NAPLES

Naples

ALBANIA

Constantinople

E M P I R E

MOREA

KINGD'M OF
SICILY

Napoleon the First invaded Russia in June 1812. At this time, Napoleon really dominated the whole of mainland Europe. Everywhere was either part of his empire or a satellite. Prussia had become a satellite, even Austria had become a satellite; all that was left of independence was Spain which was fighting against the French, and Great Britain, which was of course independent and hostile to France. Russia had been something like a satellite, although a high-minded one. The object of Napoleon's invasion of Russia was not to conquer Russia, but to win Russia's friendship back and make it once more a satellite. The remarkable thing about this war is that if you define a general war as a war in which more than two great powers take part, this was the last general war until 1914. There was not a general war in the whole of the nineteenth century, except possibly the Crimean War, which hardly counts.

But certainly, Napoleon's object was not conquest. One of his objects was to detach part of Russia. In the late eighteenth century, Poland had been partitioned, and most of Poland was now in Russia.

One of Napoleon's many objects in life was to make Poland once more an independent country, and if he had had his way in this last war, Poland would have become independent, Russia would have become dependent on Napoleon, and he really would have dominated Europe.

As it was, the more he advanced into Russia, the more silent the Russians became on the other hand. They did not make an elaborate resistance, although they kept up a resistance, but what they did was to refuse to acknowledge Napoleon's existence. Napoleon never meant to go to Moscow. He thought that once he said, 'I'm going to Moscow,' the Russians would take fright and at once give way to whatever he wanted. In past times he had always gone for the capital. Once he had got to the capital, he had won. This time he reached Moscow by September, and the first thing he said to his agents, who were

The Grand Army's invasion of Moscow

already in Moscow, was, 'Has the emissary from the Tsar arrived?' He thought: Now I'm in Moscow, Alexander will send a message of surrender. No emissary came. For a whole month, or very near it, the vast French army, probably the biggest army which had ever been mobilised in European history until that time, was scattered in and around Moscow, with conditions getting worse — Moscow burning — and at the end of September, Napoleon made his first gesture, not quite of surrender, but of retreat. He withdrew from Moscow. And the retreat from Moscow, unlike the advance, was a catastrophe.

All the way back to the frontier, the French had to fight their way. They suffered terrible casualties. The Russians suffered great casualties as well, but they seemed to have endless resources. And there was a moment when it looked as if the French were all going to be cut off when they couldn't manage to cross the Beresina. It was only the work of sappers building temporary bridges that got them back over the Beresina and out of Russia.

Napoleon's disastrous retreat across the Beresina

In December 1812, the Napoleonic empire had already begun to shake. Its prestige was going. In the middle of December, Napoleon left his army still on Russian territory, and with one associate mounted in a curious sort of box sledge in which he drove right across Europe. It took him something like a fortnight to get to Paris. And it was not until the very end of December that he announced in Paris: 'The Grand Army has been lost'. He was still confident that he could build up a new army, and in the early days of 1813, Napoleon returned to his army; he brought new forces together and in the first months of 1813 inflicted defeat on Russia and also on Prussia who, very cautiously, had now gone over to the Russian side. After these two French victories, there was again a pause, because Napoleon had no idea what to do. What was he aiming for? He was aiming for a reconciliation with Russia. But the more he defeated or challenged Russia in the field, the more unlikely the Russians were to become partners with Napoleon. He was

General Kotusov, the last of the great Russian generals

in a deadlock. His short period of victories was not followed by further new advances by the French. When they were exhausted, the Russians came back and built up new forces. Incidentally, they now cast off the military leadership of Alexander and for some time had Kotusov, the last of the great Russian generals who, however, died in March 1813.

What Napoleon wanted was negotiation. He proposed an armistice which came into force and continued for most of the first part of 1813. He said later in life, when he was on St Helena, that the greatest mistake he ever made in his life was that armistice, because during the time of the armistice his army did not increase, but the Russian and the Prussian armies did. More than that. Technically, until this moment, Austria was an ally of France. Napoleon himself was married to an Austrian arch-duchess, he'd only just been married to her, and the Emperor was his father-in-law. But now, with Russia, and to a lesser extent Prussia, appearing on the field, Austria began to waver.

There was a celebrated meeting between Napoleon and Metternich, the Austrian statesman, which went on, it is said, for nine hours. Napoleon never yielded on anything. He insisted that Russia must come back within his sphere of influence. And after these nine hours, Metternich said to Napoleon as he was going, 'Sire, you are a ruined man.' Not much later, Austria too joined in the coalition against Napoleon.

Napoleon was at his best in facing apparently difficult circumstances. And combining, or trying to combine, negotiations and renewal of war. There is another very odd thing about this war of 1812 to 1814. It was a war in which conflict was interrupted constantly by negotiations. After the meeting between Napoleon and Metternich, they agreed that there should be a European conference in Prague of all the powers involved in the war. Although desks were made, and ink pots put out, the conference never got going. But somewhat later,

*Prince Clemens
Metternich*

Frankfurt in the early nineteenth century

the conference actually moved to Frankfurt, and there they began to negotiate.

Already Napoleon was having to yield. No doubt he thought he would get it all back later. He made a supposedly generous offer that France should retain the natural frontier controlling Western Germany, and of course Italy as well, then there could be peace. At the same time as they were having peace conferences in Frankfurt, war was being resumed in Germany.

In August of 1813, the war was renewed and once more Napoleon was victorious, defeated the Prussians and even made the Russians retreat.

But these victories led to nothing, because all that happened was that the Prussians and the Russians retreated, and then when Napoleon pulled up his army *they* came back.

In October, there was the first great battle of the war — or the greatest battle since Borodino in 1812. This was when Napoleon was drawing his troops back and had to retreat

The storming of Dresden in August 1813, an impressive but not particularly useful victory for Napoleon

Later in the year, Napoleon was defeated at Leipzig and had to retreat

through Leipzig. He was confident at first that not only would he carve his way through Leipzig, but that he would inflict a defeat on the allies as, when he challenged them, he had always done. And this time, after a three-day battle, the French were defeated.

This is a landmark in European history. It was the first time, since France had become the military leader of Europe, that there was not merely a defeat, but a complete disaster to the French army. There had been disaster in Russia because of the horrible conditions of the retreat, but this was the first, the very first test in warfare when the French army suffered a vital defeat.

The French pulled through enough to be able to retreat to the Rhine, but the prestige of Napoleon was shaken and never restored. It was a turning point in European history.

11

For the Germans particularly, it became a national triumph. Prussia was the only German power which had really recovered its independence, and had put into the field an effective army. The Austrians counted for something. But, historically, the battle of Leipzig became, in German history, the battle of the nations, because it was not merely the regular forces; now volunteer forces poured in to support Prussia and the other German states in their resistance to Napoleon.

Despite the defeat of the French, the conference at Frankfurt went solemnly on with its discussions, and seemed to have reached a conclusion that France should have what were called the natural frontiers, in other words, the Alps and the Rhine. This would have left France with a good deal more territory than she had possessed before the Revolution of 1789. It was very characteristic that Napoleon, just having been defeated in battle, was confident that he would turn the scale next time, and therefore rejected the very favourable compromise which his negotiators had made for him. The Frankfurt conference broke down. Then there was a further pause, and early in 1814, Napoleon had gathered an army again together and he celebrated the opening of the year by a victory over the Russians who, having first attempted to invade France, withdrew again.

Now they were back at a peace conference once more, at a place called Châtillon, where they went over the ground and where the allies tightened up their terms. They now no longer offered the natural frontiers, but merely what were called the Old Frontiers, the frontiers which France had in 1789.

Napoleon thought this really not worth discussing. He merely allowed the conference to go on. As a weapon of war, in the two years between 1812 or the beginning of 1813 and the fall of Napoleon, international negotiations went on with an intensity for which there was very little parallel. Conference after conference; meeting and discussing and producing solutions and everyone heaving a sigh of relief, except Napoleon who, at the last minute, would repudiate them. And just as he celebrated 1813 with a victory over the Prussians, he celebrated 1814 with a victory over the Prussians and over the Russians.

Napoleon's farewell to the Empress Marie-Louise and the young Napoleon II in March 1814, before he resumed command of his army

But these were matters of ingenuity, they were not matters of greater resources. The truth is that if the allies, now including Austria, assembled all their forces, ultimately Napoleon would be beaten. But he relied on quickness of manoeuvre and he had quite a considerable record in 1814, of victories over the Prussians, over the Russians at one time, and the Austrians were so cautious and so anxious not to be defeated that they didn't attempt to invade France at all, but remained cautiously on the frontier out of the range of Napoleon's armies.

In March 1814, the Prussians reassembled their forces and prepared to march on Paris. Napoleon actually welcomed this.

For one thing, he felt he must keep the allies separate, that he could move his own army against the Prussians, and against the Russians, and then possibly against the Austrians. And he was delighted when Blücher, the Prussian general, marched on Paris, because he said, 'Now I can cut off his retreat,' and he thought the situation was going in his favour.

At this time, even the Russians speculated on the idea that it would be wiser to give up, that a compromise with Napoleon would be possible, that Napoleon could be offered, not only France of 1789 but perhaps, after all, the natural frontiers.

The thing which stiffened the resistance of the allies was the arrival of Castlereagh, the British Foreign Secretary, who had no troops to offer, but could offer what was more important — lots of money — and tempted the allies back into action.

By the end of March 1814, the Prussians were well established in Paris. Napoleon prepared his master stroke. He would march away from Paris, leave it exposed to the allies, and when they had gone into Paris, he would cut their communications, leave them high and dry, and would win after all.

And now one new factor came into play, a factor which was going to ruin Napoleon, and this was the resistance of the French marshals. The great French marshals had been at war, on and off, for something like twenty years. They had become very rich, they had become dukes and princes, they had great estates, and they did not want to fight any more. They had concentrated back in the Palace of Fontainebleau, and Napoleon arrived, having just carried out a successful manoeuvre to cut off Blücher's communications, and said, 'Now we can go into action against them.' The marshals all struck. Even Ney, who was the bravest of the brave, the man who had forced the passage of the Beresina, and who incidentally was to go over to Napoleon again at the time of the Hundred Days, even Ney said, 'Emperor, we have done too much, it must end.' This brought down Napoleon's plans completely. Napoleon shrugged the marshals off, saying, 'I can perfectly well conduct a war without all of you. As long as I am in command and have someone to send messages, I can

Napoleon at Fontainebleau, from the painting by Delaroche

win this war.' And then he received the disastrous news that one of the marshals had carried the argument further. Marshal Marmont, commander of fifty thousand men, the nearest force to Paris, had gone over to the allies. With that, Napoleon hadn't a fighting force at all.

In Paris there were fascinating developments. Alexander had arrived, and his problem was the question of whom they should recognise as a French government. He thought they might take Napoleon's son, or Napoleon's wife, or perhaps Bernadotte; but Talleyrand, who had been French Foreign Minister, and a very influential, very skilful politician, put forward the answer: the only alternative to Napoleon was the legitimate king, Louis the Eighteenth, who'd been living in England or sometimes exiled in Russia, ever since 1792. Alexander agreed and, long before the technical end of the war, Louis the Eighteenth was recognised — though it took him some time to arrive from England. Meanwhile the question arose as to what should happen to Napoleon.

Marshal Marmont, who delivered the coup de grâce *to Napoleon's hopes by taking his troops to the allied side*

Every now and again, Napoleon would reject the negotiations and say, 'Let us carry on with the war.' But after Marshal Marmont had deserted, there was really no hope that he could do so. On 3rd April 1814, he abdicated.

This was the end of the war so far as Napoleon was concerned, and you can't really say that there was ever an end to the war by means of a treaty. There was a treaty, but it was simply a stopping of the fight, because the person who fought was no longer in power. The only agreement that was made was an agreement between the allied powers and the former Emperor Napoleon, making him emperor of Elba.

The great Napoleonic empire had come to an end. And instead there followed one of the most curious peace treaties in the record of modern times: a peace treaty with Louis the Eighteenth. But the allies had never been fighting Louis the Eighteenth. He had been in exile and had claimed to be king from 1795 onwards. Now he was king, but there was no way in which the allies could make a peace treaty with him because they had never been at war with him. What followed was, probably, the most generous peace treaty ever made by victors regarding a country that had been such a nuisance to them. France was not asked to pay any indemnity, she was not asked to return any of the works of art which Napoleon had plundered, she was not asked to reduce her army, and she was even allowed to take some of the territory which the French Revolution had gathered. France returned to the ranks of the great powers without any atonement, because it was a different France.

This was not quite the end of the story. Eighteen months later, Napoleon had another go; he returned for the Hundred Days. But he was quickly defeated at Waterloo and withdrew. Just to make the record complete, the second peace of Paris was a little harsher. France had to pay a small indemnity and, in particular, had to return the works of art. And that is why the four horses of St Mark are on St Mark's church in Venice and not in the Louvre in France.

The Piazza San Marco, with one of the four horses of St Mark

II

THE CONGRESS OF VIENNA
1815

Europe after the Congress of Vienna 1815

0	100	200	miles
100	300	km	

New Republics and/or restored Monarchies   PARMA

Boundary of the German Confederation

Austro-Hungarian Empire

NORTH SEA

DENM.

Sc

OLDENBURG   HC

UNITED
KINGDOM

London

KINGDOM OF NETHERLANDS

HA

WEST-
PHALI

BELGIUM

Rhine

Paris

Lorraine

ATLANTIC OCEAN

FRANCE

Alsace

SWITZ.

KINGDOM OF

Savoy   Pied
mont

SARDINIA

PAF

MODE

Toulon

TUS

SPAIN

Madrid

Corsica

Lisbon

PORTUGAL

KINGDOM
OF
SARDINIA

When Napoleon fell, in April 1814, there was no independent authority in Europe; for some years everything in Europe had turned on Napoleon. The only state on the continent of any magnitude was of course Russia. That was why Napoleon had gone to Moscow so unsuccessfully. Great Britain was really independent, but she was not on the continent of Europe. Suddenly the Europe that had known so many changes was left alone to be arranged. The four allies — Russia, Austria, Prussia and Great Britain — decided that a *great* congress should be held in order to settle the future of Europe.

The invitations were sent out by the Emperor of Austria. The four allies held a preliminary meeting in Vienna at the beginning of October 1814. They were just beginning to settle down on an agenda and what they would decide, when the door opened and Talleyrand, the French Foreign Minister, came in and expressed surprise at seeing them. He said, 'Who are you?' They said, 'We are the four great allies.' 'Not at all,' he said, 'the alliance came to an end the moment Napoleon signed the treaty of peace and abdicated. So it must be, simply, the great powers. France is a great power, so I'm going to sit in with you, and as a matter of fact, I've brought the representatives of Spain, Portugal and Sweden, as well, that makes up the eight who are the great European powers. We won't bother much about Poland.' In fact the Spaniard was a great nuisance too. But the character of the meeting was changed, because here were delegates who had not been involved as an alliance, but representing the independence of many countries.

The conference worked partly with committees, partly with the direction of the great five, and partly by ideas being put up. Some things the Congress leaders were quite clear about. They did not like republics. They restored most of the monarchs who were knocking around Vienna. A lot of them were not much good as monarchs, but all the same, they had the title of king or grand-duke or arch-duke, and they had been dethroned by Napoleon, so here they were put back again. But where Napoleon had destroyed a republic, the directors of the Congress of Vienna did not restore it. Out of the three hundred free cities in Germany, the great majority disappeared. In fact,

Isabey's painting of the Congress of Vienna

before long, there were only two free cities left in Germany. Frankfurt was one, Hamburg was the other, and Hamburg has retained some of the characteristics of a free city to the present day.

In Italy, the prejudice against republics was even more striking. Venice, Venezia, was a state far older than most of the monarchies or grand-duchies of Italy, but because it was a republic, it was simply given to Austria, and lost its independence forever. The same thing happened to Genoa, which was incorporated in the Kingdom of Sardinia.

When they met, there was one problem which the Congress leaders had not contemplated. It was the problem which, in a sense, caused Napoleon to go to Moscow — the problem of Poland. And now, with Napoleon gone, the problem of Poland raised its head. Until the year 1772, Poland was a great, independent state, not very well run; with an elective monarch,

Talleyrand, the French Foreign Minister

usually the elector of Saxony, but still elected in a confused way; and while the neighbours of Poland — Russia, Prussia and Austria — had grown stronger, Poland had grown weaker.

In 1772 there was a partition of most of Poland. Russia took the central part, Prussia took one of the edges, Austria took

Galicia. There was a further partition in 1792 and a final partition in 1795 when Poland disappeared altogether. But there was still a sense of Polish nationalism. And in 1809 Napoleon resurrected a small independent Poland as the Grand Duchy of Warsaw.

Alexander had cast himself as a new saviour of Poland. What he wanted was to resurrect a kingdom of Poland which would include the whole of Poland, would all be under him as Protector and Tsar, in fact would be a Russian satellite state — a phrase which you may have heard suggested in more recent times. The others obviously did not like this.

Nevertheless, when the great powers first met, Alexander was much the most powerful in armies, in background, and in the fact that he'd been able to fight Napoleon and defeat him. More than any other, it was Russian armies which defeated Napoleon and, if you like, liberated Europe.

Now Alexander was threatening to use this same great army in order to impose his will. Prussia was quite prepared to fit in. Prussia would surrender — hand over her share of Poland — if the king of Prussia could have Saxony instead. And there was a good argument for this, because the king of Saxony had stayed with Napoleon too late and was still an ally of Napoleon when Napoleon fell. So obviously he wasn't entitled to keep his kingdom, or so it appeared. But there he was; hanging around Vienna, hoping to insert himself.

In the autumn of 1814, it looked as if the Congress of Vienna was going to break up in dispute. And then a very sensational thing happened. Talleyrand raised his head again.

On 2nd January 1815, Talleyrand, without any authority from his government, signed on behalf of France an alliance with Great Britain and Austria against Russia. Whether it would have ever operated, whether the French armies would have marched, whether the British and Austrian armies would

One of the results of the Congress of Vienna (seen top left) *was the disappearance of several republics for good, notably Venice and Genoa*

27

*The Emperor
Alexander I*

ever have worked together, we cannot say. But it was enough
to do the trick. In the course of the spring of 1815 Alexander
compromised and finally agreed that while he was entitled to
resurrect Poland in the share that he had received in the
original partitions, Austria would retain her share, Galicia
(which she retained until the end of the Austrian empire), and
Prussia would retain her share of Poland (which Prussia, or
alternatively Germany afterwards, retained until 1945, if not
later).

There still was a sort of kingdom of Poland because although
Poland was now only the central part of Poland under Russian
control, it was still given a Polish character. Indeed, from 1815
to 1830, Poland had an autonomous government. The brother
of Tsar Alexander, Grand-Duke Constantine, acted as Viceroy

Alexander's brother, Grand-Duke Constantine, the enthusiastic Viceroy of Poland

of Poland, married a Polish countess and thought of himself as more Polish than Russian.

In 1825 when Alexander died, or is supposed to have died, Constantine the next heir refused the Russian throne because he said, 'I wanted to stay as ruler of Poland.' And it was the next heir, Tsar Nicholas, who became the tyrant of Russia from then until the Crimean War. There is a curious little point about Alexander. He went on tour in Southern Russia in 1825, he developed a serious illness and then, presumably, he died. He was buried at a place in Southern Russia where a tomb was erected. And in 1855, when they opened the tomb, there was nothing there. Legend has it that Alexander abdicated his throne and became a hermit. Members of the Imperial house used regularly to go down to Southern Russia to sit at the feet of this hermit until he died in the due course of nature. How much truth there is in this story I've not the slightest idea. I suspect none, but what happened to Alexander's body we shall never know.

The Polish affair was the great crisis of the Congress of Vienna. It was settled peacefully and Alexander was able to reassert his leadership over the Congress by presenting a plan of his own that the allies, indeed all those who were associated with the Congress of Vienna, should continue to maintain a system of co-operation and to recognise an all-European organisation.

Alexander wanted to build this on high Christian principles and indeed called it the Holy Alliance: a resurrection of the Holy Roman empire which had existed in Germany in the Middle Ages. The Holy Alliance not only took high-minded religious views, it took strong political views. In other words, that really good Christians did not believe in constitutional governments or in the control of absolute monarchs. This was not a theme which was at all acceptable to the British government, or for that matter, to Castlereagh, the British delegate.

The Holy Alliance put forward the framework, for the first time since the Middle Ages, of how states should co-operate together, in particular with an implication that if any monarch was in trouble from liberalism, from constitutionalism, the other members of the Holy Alliance would come to his assistance.

In the first few years, after the Congress of Vienna, much of its work seemed satisfactory. There were liberal movements in Germany, which were arrested within the German confederation, under the guidance of Metternich. There were liberal conspiracies in Italy, particularly in Naples where indeed the Austrian army ultimately intervened. After the first few years, it seemed that the Congress of Vienna had established a firm, lasting Europe and that the Holy Alliance was an essential part of it

Lord Castlereagh

which brought the conservative powers of Europe together and made them a formidable force.

In 1819 there was a second congress at Aix-la-Chapelle which people nowadays call Aachen. It dealt with fairly routine things, but some much to the good. It arranged for the withdrawal of the foreign armies which had, after the Hundred Days, occupied France. It also terminated the payment of an indemnity from France to the allies and made France a completely independent country, and one which was recognised for good and all as one of the five great powers.

Later there was a congress about giving a blessing to Austria for intervening in Naples. And then there came something they hadn't expected — there was a liberal movement in Spain. And with this liberal movement there were the beginnings of a civil war. Alexander at once claimed that here was the great opportunity for the Holy Alliance. There should be a strong military intervention against the liberal leaders in Spain, and

*The withdrawal of the Prussians from Paris after the Congress
of Aix-la-Chapelle*

the strong intervention should be provided by the Russian army. This did not meet with British approval at all. Not for the first time and certainly not for the last, the British government took the view that if there was a liberal government out of hand somewhere, it should be allowed to lead its country to destruction, but there should not be an intervention by the great powers against this liberal movement.

After a lot of controversy, they had yet another congress, this time at Verona. It was the last. Castlereagh was now dead and the Duke of Wellington, a somewhat taciturn man, was the British delegate. When it came to his turn, he just said, 'My instructions are that we're against intervention in Spain'. And every time the discussion went round and it came to him, he just said, 'Against.' This wrecked the congress. Not only did Verona not arrive at any firm conclusion, but the congress system, as it was set up in 1815, and as people had anticipated it would go on and on, broke down. The old congress, as envisaged in the Holy Alliance, never met after 1822.

As a matter of fact, a very simple way of dealing with the Spanish liberals was then discovered. It was found that Great Britain had no objection if a neighbouring state intervened. The French at that time being very conservative and also somewhat anxious to use their army which had been out of work ever since 1815, intervened in Spain and restored the absolute monarchy. The British made no complaint and Spain went on its peculiar way which led to a great many liberal governments in Spain during the nineteenth century and also to a great many risings of resistance against these liberal governments and a confused history of Spain throughout the nineteenth century. But the decisive thing which happened in 1822 is that the congress system broke down.

Alexander provided a certain element of high morality for another two or three years but then disappeared off the scene.

The 'balance of Europe', as it was called, had been created. England and France represented, sometimes they call it the Liberal Alliance, sometimes simply the Western Alliance; they were able to throw their own weight into the balance against Russia. But by this time Russia had lost interest, particularly

The French army was permitted to intervene in Spain, as France was a neighbouring state: the taking of the Trocadero

under Nicholas, in European affairs. It was a landmark when Alexander died. He had been an obsessive European; Nicholas was a Russian, and when he turned his interest to foreign affairs he was interested in the near East, in Turkey.

He intervened in Turkey more than once, finally being led into the Crimean War, where one sees a perfect pattern of west and east. The two western powers, England and France, opposed Russia, the eastern power, over the question of Turkey. They fought a rather futile, ill-planned war, the Crimean War, which though it led to the defeat of Russia, did not change the situation at all, except that Russia was somewhat weaker. But there is one thing worth mentioning about the Crimean War, because here was a last echo of the Congress of Vienna.

When England and France, the two western, supposedly

Tsar Nicholas I

liberal powers went to war against Russia, the revolutionaries of Europe urged them to take the war, not only into Turkey, but into continental Europe by raising the standard of a free Poland; and though that standard was never raised between 1854 and 1856, there was something like a Polish revolution and an attempt to restore free Poland in the Polish rising of 1863.

More remotely, the Italian revolutionaries had a fantasy that Italy could be liberated as a result of the Crimean War. Indeed, they hoped for some sort of congress, and they were right. One of the rare congresses was held in Paris in 1856. It was a sort of thin resurrection of the Congress of Vienna. It laid down quite a lot of international law, particularly maritime law about when ships could be arrested at sea, and things of this kind. This was not welcome to Great Britain which wanted to extend British naval power all over the world. It was

The defence of Sebastopol during the Crimean War, 1854-55

supported by France but it did not go very far. Nevertheless, the Congress of Paris did achieve something. There was one other congress which also sprang out of the eastern question. When Russia once more went to war with Turkey in 1877, the whole thing was wound up by a congress at Berlin in 1878, where there was a great European gathering and where, incidentally, Disraeli, Lord Beaconsfield made a great speech, or so it was said. He was proposing to speak in French. Lord Salisbury had to persuade him to speak in English because he said, 'Everyone is wanting to hear your wonderful English oratory.' What Salisbury and other English people did not want to hear was Disraeli's dreadful French.

That was the last congress until after the first World War. The Congress of Berlin stands out because, in the whole history of the nineteenth century, after the Congress of Vienna, it was the one time when all the great powers came together and reached some conclusions of value.

The Congress of Paris in 1856: Lord Clarendon signs

The Congress of Berlin in 1878 to restore a balance to south-eastern Europe: Disraeli standing, sixth from left, *and* Bismarck, centre

III

THE FIRST WORLD WAR: ARMISTICE

The Great War, as it was called at the time, what we now call the First World War, curiously started without any war aims except, of course, to win. It wasn't until the end of 1916 that the German Chancellor put forward a public pronouncement that the combatants should meet to settle the war, and he had already defined his war aims, though he did not tell anyone what he was going to ask, which was simply that Germany should keep forever all the territory which she had overrun, including Belgium and most of northern France. The following month Lloyd George also talked about a settlement of war aims, but what he meant was that the Germans should give up everything they had conquered and pay a good deal of compensation into the bargain. So war aims had rather got stuck, and it was not for some time later that anyone discussed seriously how the war should end.

1917 was the first time when general public opinion moved towards the idea that there should be a discussion and a settlement of war. In August 1917 the German Reichstag, which had broken with Bethmann and was moving to the Left, carried a peace resolution. This was the first formal time when the idea of discussing peace was considered. There was no response from the allies, although they in their turn were worrying that they must bring the war to an end somehow. The other great change which happened in 1917 and raised the question of war aims was the entry of the United States into the war, because from the very first the United States had been fighting for some wider aims than merely victory, because if they wanted victory they could just stay out. They had to stand for something, and this was President Wilson's first attempt to formulate war aims, which he did entirely differently from his associates. The United States was never an ally but simply an associated power, and Wilson felt that he should decide the settlement of the war without considering what England and France felt about it. This was the first occasion when this arose. What happened in 1917 was a development of public opinion rather than a statesmanlike activity.

In the summer of 1917, when the German Social Democrats were getting influential, they proposed a meeting of all

A steamship sinks after being hit by a shell from a German submarine

Socialists or representatives of all Socialist Parties at Stockholm. The Germans were able to go and the Russians were able to go because they had just had a revolution. Neither the British nor the French Socialists were allowed to go: the French Socialists were forbidden by their Government, the British Socialists who were such moderate persons as Ramsay MacDonald and Henderson, were simply not carried by the sailors. They said, 'Whenever we go to sea our ships are sunk by German submarines — we're not going to have anyone going talking to them.' So the Stockholm conference did not affect people very widely. Still, there was an assertion that something should be done about ending the war, and indeed this was the first time that there was something like a serious discussion. The new Emperor Charles of Austria-Hungary, the Habsburg monarch who had succeeded Franz Josef in November 1916, put forward proposals for ending the war. He never got down to direct negotiations, this was done at second hand. What he proposed was that Austria-Hungary should act as a mediator and should be rewarded by being given a large slice of Poland, in general conducting the negotiations as though it was a completely impartial power. The Emperor Charles said he hoped to be able to get Alsace and Lorraine for France, giving away, one might say, German territory without ever asking the Germans.

As soon as this story reached the ears of the Germans, they protested and Charles backed down. But it had an effect on both the British and French Governments. Throughout 1917 there were constant efforts to come back to Emperor Charles and to stir him up, to encourage his pacific thoughts. He had pacific thoughts all right but when it came to a programme he ran up against the obstacle that anything he proposed would

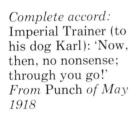

Complete accord: Imperial Trainer (to his dog Karl): 'Now, then, no nonsense; through you go!' *From* Punch *of May 1918*

have to be forced on the Germans and they were much too strong for him. There was a time when the western allies said to Charles, 'We're quite prepared to make peace with you if you join with us, or let us through Austria, to invade Germany from the south.' But this would have meant war between Germany and Austria-Hungary and although the emperor was certainly stating ideas, indeed Charles had them all ready, Germany was too strong for him; so that although this business of Austrian negotiations ran on as late as the summer of 1918 and General Smuts, a member of the British War Cabinet, was in Switzerland negotiating with an Austrian delegate, nothing came of it.

In 1917 Russia had a revolution, at first a moderate, democratic revolution and then, in November 1917, the Bolshevik revolution which put the Bolsheviks in power as

October 1917: soldiers and students lying in wait for the police by the Moika Canal in St Petersburg

Early days: Stalin, Lenin and Trotsky

they remain to the present day. The Bolsheviks, Lenin in particular, held a clear view that if he offered no indemnities and no annexations, this would capture public opinion in the democratic countries of the west. In any case, he simply declared that the war with Germany was at an end; he said, 'We're not going to fight it any more.' There was then an attempt at a peace conference. It was held in Brest Litovsk, then in Russia, later in Poland, and it ran over the whole winter. Trotsky made his reputation there for the first time because he argued persistently with the Germans that any attempts to annex Russian territory were against democratic principles and the wider principles that the Germans themselves claimed to support. In the end the negotiations simply broke down because though Trotsky could argue much better than the Germans did, the answers particularly of the representatives of the German General Staff were to say, 'Well, we don't care whether what we're doing is right or wrong, we're going to do it, and we're going to take a lot of Russian territory.' Trotsky then hit on another solution — as he thought — where he simply said, 'We proclaim neither peace nor war. We stop fighting but we are not going to make a peace with you because you're asking too much. So I just announce the war is over. Good morning.'

45

And he went back to Moscow. He calculated that the German High Command would not have the nerve to break off peaceful relations and march further into Russia. He was wrong. The German army began to roll forward. Lenin, who had always foreseen this, insisted that Trotsky must go back to Brest Litovsk and sign the Robbers' Treaty, which he did. Russia lost a lot of territory. As things turned out it was for a comparatively short space of time. But sensationally one part of the war was over, that is to say Germany was no longer fighting Russia and the German army was not needed in the east — though as a matter of fact it was needed to hold down the difficult peoples of European Russia. But it left Germany free for a last offensive, and from March 1918 until August, the Germans were rolling forward and many people anticipated a complete defeat for England and France.

In August things turned the other way. The Germans had run out of strength, and when the allies, that is to say Haig and the French Commander in Chief, sent their armies forward they achieved something that they had never done in the preceding three years: they broke through. From August

German infantry pursuing bands of Bolsheviks in the Ukraine, Autumn 1917

*The rejuvenated German advance: infantry advancing over a
captured trench, June 1918*

onwards the allied armies were advancing, driving the Germans
back, and the Germans very soon would have to anticipate
complete defeat. Meanwhile the German front was collapsing
in the east. In September 1918 Bulgaria made peace, which
meant that the allies could roll forward into southern Austria-
Hungary and that the Austrians too were facing collapse. This
was very sensational. On 29th September Ludendorff's nerve
broke. He said that the Germans must make an armistice at
once.

By this time there had been an advance towards democracy
in Germany and a democratic Chancellor called Prince Max of
Baden. Prince Max insisted that they should approach the

President Woodrow Wilson in 1918

United States first because he said, 'If we can settle the United States it doesn't matter about the others, but we will negotiate with them not on terms of an armistice but on general terms for the future.' And for nearly a month the Germans and President Wilson negotiated. Wilson had devised a whole set of peace principles called 'The Fourteen Points' and did not bother to consult the associated powers. Indeed, when he had got the Germans to accept the Fourteen Points, as he did at the end of October, he assumed that the Allies would accept them too. There were bitter meetings of the allied leaders, the British, the French, the Italians. When they first met, Clemenceau, the French Premier, said to Lloyd George, 'Do you know what the Fourteen Points are?' Lloyd George said, 'I've never read them.' But in the two or three days that were left to them they had to go through these points, decide on them. In theory, of course, the allies were as much committed to the Fourteen Points as the Americans were, because Wilson had put them out. There remained the armistice to settle. This too was negotiated with President Wilson, and when the time came for the allies to settle the armistice — it was Foch particularly who conducted the armistice negotiations — there again he had not known what the terms were that President Wilson had agreed with the Germans, he just had to accept them.

Meanwhile there was a revolution in Germany. The Kaiser was overthrown and a government of Social Democrats was established which accepted the principle that at once the war must be brought to an end. But this was only part of what happened in Europe.

The main decision certainly was between Germany and the conflicting powers, but the European war during the past two or three years had spread more widely. Firstly there was Austria-Hungary fighting both in the Balkans and in Italy and then there was Turkey, or the Ottoman Empire, involved in fighting in Europe and also in Asia, and up until now they had been kept in line by the Germans. There was a gradual breakdown of German powers. Up to September 1918 Austria-Hungary, and the Turks for that matter, imagined that if they were in difficulty German forces could come to help them. By September of 1918 Germany had not the forces with which to assist her allies. Everything was breaking down and the allies of Germany had to face their own problem of making armistice, which they did with whichever of the allies happened to be on

49

the spot. For instance, the Sultan of Turkey made an armistice with the commander of a British battleship which got up to Constantinople when the Straits became opened. The armistice was duly signed, but Clemenceau was furious at this and said the Sultan should have signed with France as well. So the armistice was cancelled until a French battleship could go up to Constantinople so that the Sultan, or his representative, could sign their armistice too.

The first formal armistice between the allies and what were called the Central Powers was at the end of September when Bulgaria signed with the French commander and opened the door, as Ludendorff complained, to the allied armies. By the beginning of October the whole situation was moving towards a German collapse, with the additional factor that the Habsburg monarchy of Austria-Hungary not only agreed to armistices with its various contending allied forces, but collapsed — it broke altogether. Earlier in the year when the British and French had been asked about a war aim, they had replied, 'One of our war aims is national self-determination' — that every area which was inhabited by a separate nationality could claim its own national state. This was a tremendous encouragement to the nationalities of Austria-Hungary and as soon as the chance came, at the end of October, the Czechs proclaimed the Czechoslovak Republic and the Croats, Slovenes and Serbs all put themselves under the authority of the King of Serbia in a federation which became Yugoslavia. Finally in October the Italians negotiated with Austria-Hungary and on 3rd November the Austrian commander in Italy, because he was fighting still on Italian soil, signed an armistice of complete surrender. The Austrian armies broke up. The soldiers went back as best they could. Austria-Hungary ceased to exist and what remained, on 10th November, was the Austrian Republic, the republic which still exists. (This was not the end of the break-up for Austria-Hungary. In November the French armies operating from Salonika reached the frontiers of Hungary and imposed a stern, crushing armistice on the new republican state of Hungary because Hungary was regarded as an ally of Germany, not one of the peoples struggling to be free. This was quite wrong.)

Revolution in Berlin: note the machine gun, also the hand grenade in the sailor's belt

Back to November 1918: the Germans accepted that they would seek for an armistice. The situation was very confused. There was a revolution in Berlin, there was fighting in the streets. Somehow a peace delegation was got together. It crossed the allied lines in the dark and was confronted in a railway carriage at Rethonde with the allied Commander in Chief, Marshal Foch. Foch is reputed to have asked, 'What are these persons doing here?' and the officer who brought them in said, 'They've come to seek an armistice', to which Foch merely said, '*Très bien.*' He then dictated the terms. There was no clear negotiation, simply a statement of terms, and the German delegation was in no position to turn them down. Erzberger, the leader of the delegation, attempted to make some impression and to say that with the terrible conditions of food

51

The arrival of the train for the signing of the armistice

shortage in Germany, he hoped that as soon as the armistice was signed food supplies could be sent through to the German people. His request was ignored.

There was one other aspect. Foch and his staff negotiated without any authority on behalf of all the allied powers, particularly of course of Great Britain, and for that matter of Belgium, and even the United States. There was one non-French representative, Admiral Wemyss, who spoke for the British because they attached importance to the surrender of the German fleet, and this was inserted as one of the terms of the armistice.

The negotiations for the armistice took about eight days. First of all the German delegation had to hear it all, then they had to take it back to Berlin, then they had to come back. It was only at 11 o'clock on 11th November that the armistice actually came into force. And when it came into force it was one of a great number. Broadly, the fighting stopped all over Europe and indeed all over Asia Minor. It did not mean that the fighting stopped for long. Already British and French troops were moving into Russia and preparing for the war of intervention against the Bolsheviks which they tried to conduct ineffectually until 1921. But in this hugger-mugger of a way a war which had started in confusion, with no clear definition at

The surrender of the German fleet, November 1918: British warships lead the way

the beginning of what the war aims were, ended with no clear idea of war aims either. Everything was passed over to the great peace conference in Paris which was to follow in 1919 and to make a new world. Whether they succeeded in that is a different matter, but what is certain is that with the general signature of armistice the Great War was over and with it the connection of Europe with its past.

The 9th East Surreys cheer the news of the armistice on the Western front

Celebrations in London's East End

IV

THE FIRST WORLD WAR: THE PEACE CONFERENCE

NORWAY

Oslo

SWEDEN

Stockholm

FINLAND

Helsinki

Lake Ladoga

St Petersburg
(Petrograd)

NORTH SEA

UNITED
KINGDOM

BALTIC SEA

Riga

Memel

RUSSIAN

EMPIRE

Smolensk

Königsberg

Vilna

NETHERLANDS

Ypres

BELGIUM.

Brussels

Amiens

Mons

Laon

Rheims

Paris

Verdun

Metz

Strasbourg

Saarbrücken

P R U S S I A

Rhine

Berlin

G E R M A N Y

Leipzig

Dresden

Breslau

Tannenberg

Warsaw

Brest Litovsk

Kiev

Dnieper

Elbe

Seine

Marne

F R A N C E

Rhone

Lyons

Basel

SWITZ.

Milan

B A V A R I A

Danube

Munich

Prague

BOHEMIA

Tyrol

Trentino

A U S T R I A

AUSTRO-

HUNGARIAN

EMPIRE

Vienna

Budapest

H U N G A R Y

TRANSYLVANIA

Cracow

GALICIA

Lemberg

Dniester

BESSARABIA

M O L D A V I A

Prut

Odess

Po

Venice

Trieste

Istria

CROATIA

BOSNIA

Sarajevo

Danube

Belgrade

R U M A N I A

Bucharest

Wallachia

Dobruja

Corsica

Rome

ADRIATIC SEA

MONTENEGRO

S E R B I A

BULGARIA

Sofia

BLACK

SEA

Constantinople

Naples

ALBANIA

MACEDONIA

Salonica

T U R K E Y

Gallipoli

Sardinia

I T A L Y

GREECE

OTTOMAN
EMPIRE

Europe in 1914

————— Boundary of the Central Powers at the outbreak of the First World War

Boundary of the Austro-Hungarian Empire

(Bulgaria and Turkey subsequently joined the Central Powers)

0   100   200
| | | miles
100   300 | km

NORWAY

Oslo

SWEDEN

Stockholm

FINLAND

Helsinki

Lake Ladoga

Leningrad

ESTONIA

U. S. S. R.

NORTH SEA

Riga

LATVIA

UNITED
KINGDOM

Copenhagen

BALTIC SEA

Memel

LITHUANIA

Königsberg

Vilna

WHITE
RUSSIA

Free City
of Danzig

EAST
PRUSSIA

NETHERLANDS

Elbe

Berlin

G E R M A N Y

Poznan

Brest Litovsk

Brussels

BELGIUM

Cologne

Warsaw

P O L A N D

Luxembourg

Rhine

Saar

Dresden

Breslau

Lublin

Lvov

UKRAINE

Dnieper

Lorraine

Prague

C Z E C H O S L O V A K I A

Marne

Alsace

Danube

Bohemia

Moravia

Dniester

Seine

Munich

Vienna

Slovakia

BESSARABIA

FRANCE

Bern

SWITZ.

Tyrol

A U S T R I A

HUNGARY

Budapest

R U M A N I A

Odessa

Rhône

Trentino

Milan

Po

Trieste

Y
U
G
O
S
L
A
V
I
A

Belgrade

Bucharest

BLACK

SEA

Corsica

I T A L Y

ADRIATIC SEA

Danube

B U L G A R I A

Constantinople
(Istanbul)

Rome

Sofia

Sardinia

Naples

ALBANIA

Tirana

Salonika

T
U
R
K
E
Y

GREECE

Sicily

Europe after the Peace Treaty of Versailles

0   100   200
                miles
                km
100   300

The Paris Peace Conference of 1919 was the most ambitious peace conference there had ever been to date, although it has been eclipsed in later days. It was a conference not only to settle one peace, the peace with Germany, but to make peace with all the powers and to deal with a lot of things that were never involved in the war at all. People often refer to the peace settlement as the Settlement of Versailles. That really is technically wrong. The peace conference met in Paris, it met all over the place, wherever they could get people into committee rooms; but when they were actually having the signature of a peace treaty, they needed some bigger assembly hall, somewhere that Paris could not provide. The French, fortunately, had a number of palaces scattered round Paris, and they took over one of these for the day. The most important was, of course, the peace treaty with Germany which was signed at Versailles. So one is entitled to refer to the Treaty of Versailles, but one is not entitled to refer to the Congress or Conference of Versailles.

There were plenty of other moves out to palaces. The peace treaty with little Austria was signed at Saint Germain, the peace treaty with a very much curtailed Hungary was signed at the Trianon. The peace treaty with Bulgaria was signed at Neuilly and the peace treaty with Turkey would have been signed at Sèvres, but they never got it off the ground as a peace treaty because the Turks turned against it.

Another interesting point — the peace conference of 1919 was not a congress even though far more people attended it than attended the earlier congresses. The difference is this. The Paris Peace Conference drew up the peace treaties with the enemies. When a particular peace treaty was ready, the defeated foe sent delegates who turned up at a meeting, not to argue, but solely to sign the peace treaty. In other words, what met at Paris was a conference, and because the enemy was never represented at this conference, it never became a congress. In 1878, for instance, the Turks who had been defeated in the recent war turned up for the congress just as much as the Russians turned up. But no congress has ever

*The Council of Four at the Paris Peace Conference: Orlando,
Lloyd George, Clemenceau and Wilson*

been held since. In 1945 the Germans did not get much of a
look in to say what they had to say.

What we had was an enormous gathering of diplomats —
committees of all kinds, committees dealing with this point,
committees dealing with that point and a directing body which
started with about twelve foreign secretaries from the main
countries and swelled up sometimes to twenty or so. But after
the conference, which met originally in January, had been
meeting for a little while, quite without authority from anyone
except themselves, the really great men took it over and
became the directing bodies. The great men were originally the
big three — President Wilson, the most important because he

was a sovereign in himself, he was a directing power, Lloyd George who was a Prime Minister at any rate, and Clemenceau from France. After about a month or so Orlando the Italian Prime Minister, who really had not had much to do with the war except in Italy — he had never been involved in the French war — came from Italy and became one of the big four, though his standing was nothing like as great as the others. And after that again, there came a representative from Japan. This was awkward, as it made the numbers up to five. The question was raised with the Japanese: 'What will happen if the European delegates vote two each?' To which the Japanese delegate replied, very ingeniously: 'Japan always goes with the majority.' How you get a majority when it's two-all is difficult to say, but that is a course that Japan followed thereafter.

The Supreme Council, as it was called, was more than merely a negotiating body. It took over the Supreme War Council, which had run the war in its latter stages, so that it was both an executive body — deciding where armies should go to, what steps should be taken of a purely practical kind — and a negotiating body. The big three, or big four, were not very well instructed, say, in the techniques of European geography. Harold Nicolson describes going to a meeting of the big four in President Wilson's private flat — that is another thing about the Supreme Council, it did not have an official meeting place, it just met in Wilson's flat — and Nicolson describes going in to give some advice to the big four and finding these great men, all men in their fifties or older, crawling about over the floor, studying maps and discovering places they had never heard of before, of which they were going to decide the fate, move the frontiers and do things of this kind.

Their predominant problem, it was true, was peace with Germany. Germany was the only great power among the enemy powers. Austria-Hungary had been a great power, but it had dissolved into pieces: it had become Austria, a republic, Hungary, another republic (and at that moment a left-wing republic, at that), and then new states which had been carved out of the old Austrian empire, particularly Czechoslavakia and Yugoslavia, much of which had been Austrian.

Harold Nicolson

Hungary had not ranked as a great power, but it had been a significant power. It lost far more territory than it should have lost because whenever one of the succession states, as they were called, claimed Hungarian territory, it got it, even though it was inhabited by Czechs or Rumanians — when the Hungarians tried to put up the same case, they were pushed aside as former enemies. But the basic question was to make a peace treaty with Germany. The determining factor was the series of principles which Wilson had laid down just before America

*Béla Kun, the leading figure in the first Hungarian workers'
government, addressing factory workers in April 1919*

entered the war — the Fourteen Points. These were to lay
down a pattern not only for the world, for the League of
Nations and so on, but particularly for dealings with Germany.
The Germans, in September 1918, had accepted them. The
allies had not been told of them at all until about a fortnight
before the war ended and both England and France made some
— though not very important — reservations about them.
When they got to the Peace Conference they just tried to avoid
them altogether. The first thing they had to deal with Germany
was to determine the new frontiers. It was quite easy for
France to recover Alsace and Lorraine, which indeed she did,
without ever making a peace treaty. The French said: 'It's

Delegates in session at Versailles

always been ours, and we'll just move into it.' The problem of German frontiers lay on the eastern side.

A considerable problem of the Peace Conference takes us straight back to the peace congress of 1814. What was the main problem of 1814? It was whether Poland should be resurrected. What was the predominant or a predominant problem of the Peace Conference of 1919 and 1920? It was not so much whether Poland should be resurrected, the allies had agreed that that was to happen, but what territories should Poland have? Should it have solely the territory inhabited by Poles or was it entitled to go back to the earlier, say seventeenth-century, frontiers and claim vast territories which Poland had occupied? The Polish question was to give, before the conference ended, the most acute problems and bring the allies nearest to war again.

There were other territories which were lost to Germany — a bit of territory to Belgium, a bit of territory to Denmark, but the main consideration was two-fold.

One — the allies, the British and the French, had ended the war with a promise that Germany should be made to pay. Pay what? Pay street damages which the Germans had caused? Pay on a high grade of penalties? Or simply pay all the costs of the war, including what it had cost to England, France, America and anybody else? Actually the Americans did not ask for the costs of the war, but the British did and the French still more and then the Belgians took the view that they had been particularly badly treated because Germany invaded them without any excuse whatsoever and that they ought to be compensated down to the last franc.

Lloyd George leaving the palace of Versailles after signing the treaty

Then, two, there was a problem which took up a lot of time and negotiation. War criminals should be punished. But what are war criminals? War criminals are leaders on the other side who have not so much caused the war as lost it. That is why war criminals get punished. They do not get punished because they started the war, they get punished because they were fools enough to lose it. In 1919 the allies had one chief criminal, the ex-Kaiser who had taken refuge in Holland. The Dutch refused to release him. The allies talked of banning Holland, occupying Holland, blockading Holland. The Dutch just said, 'We do not surrender the Kaiser.' And after two or three years of argument, they did not surrender him, but it was put in the treaty that he was a supreme war criminal. There were trials in Germany of a few war criminals that amounted to nothing.

Indemnities took up a lot of discussion. And then there was a discussion as to whether the allies should dictate a new form of government. Fortunately, the Germans themselves had had a revolution and had established a parliamentary republic, so the actual dictation of a form of government did not arise. There was, too, a problem associated with the distribution of territory. It was not only a matter of depriving Germany of home territory — what should happen to the German colonies? The British, in particular, held the view that they should get the German colonies on a very simple principle: when Great Britain goes to war, she always gets some colonies. The British, therefore, invented the idea that the Germans were worse at ruling colonies than they were and that they, or the Dominions as they were called, should get some of the German colonies.

Most important of all were the precautions which should be taken so that Germany could not renew the war or have a second world war. And precautions were of two kinds. One, the actual size of the German army was restricted to, altogether, a hundred thousand men, and the armaments were restricted — no tanks, no aircraft and so on. The other precaution that was taken was that the whole of West Germany, that is to say Germany up to the Rhine and in certain cases beyond, was put under allied occupation. The Treaty of Versailles did not speculate how long, though it did suggest it would be for

The German battleship Bayern, *one of 71 warships which the Germans scuttled at Scapa Flow after the allies ordered the surrender of the German navy*

fifteen or twenty-five years. Then there was something else very important from the British point of view — not only was the German navy to be surrendered (and it was surrendered so whole-heartedly that the Germans then sank it just at the time when the peace treaty was being signed), but the Germans were to have no more navy, at any rate until the peace treaty could be revised in ten or twenty years.

These were some of the things which were discussed by the Supreme Council, and in time they got a peace treaty ready and finally they had an elaborate ceremonial at the Palace of Versailles. When the German delegates came in, they were told that they could not make any reply, though in fact one of them made a short speech, just saying more or less that the loser has to have a peace treaty imposed on him and that the Germans signed purely after protest. The most symbolic act at the Peace Conference was the signing of this extraordinary document. One could not call it a peace treaty; it was a treaty calculated to provoke the Germans and lead them to work for a wholesale revision of the treaty and a restoration of Germany back into the ranks of civilised nations.

At the same time President Wilson was very anxious indeed to get the League of Nations going. Indeed he made it a condition with his allies that they should draw up a charter of the League of Nations before they did anything else, and that it should be the first clause in the German peace treaty, because the German peace treaty would be the first to be signed, and therefore he could get the League of Nations in first.

The curious situation is that although Wilson always thought highly about the treaty, he had not thought about it in practical terms and he had no draft of how it should be constituted — no constitution, no rules, no charter altogether of the League of Nations. Wilson was hopeless about this, saying, 'Well, we must . . . when can we do this?' when the British Foreign Secretary said, 'Oh, we went into this at the beginning of the war, we drew up a charter of the League of Nations and here it is.' So what, in fact, Wilson imposed on the world was a draft League of Nations which had been prepared by the British really under quite different circumstances.

It was regarded by Wilson, and by many people at the time, as the greatest step forward. The principle of the League of Nations was to bring all the powers together and to lead to international affairs being carried out not only by negotiation, but through the instrumentality of the League of Nations which would gradually make rivalry, hostility, between the independent states unnecessary and unlikely. At any rate, if one was to say what people thought at the time was the really sensational thing about the Paris Peace Conference, they would

The makers of the League of Nations: 1. Viscount Ghinda (Japan); 2. M. Bourgeois (France); 3. Lord Robert Cecil (Great Britain); 4. Signor Orlando (Italy); 5. Mr Venizelos (Greece); 6. Col. House (USA); 7. Mr Vesnitch (Serbia); 8. General Smuts (Great Britain); 9. President Wilson (USA); 10. M. Hymans (Belgium); 11. His Excellency Wellington Koo (China)

not have said, I think, the Treaty of Versailles — that was something that was bound to happen, that you take it out on the Germans — but the League of Nations, which was to bring something quite new and quite special. The great powers directed the League of Nations. There was a League of Nations Council composed of the greater powers, and then an Assembly with all the lesser ones . . . the greater powers were, it was supposed, committed to support the League of Nations and somehow to solve the problem of enforcing the declarations of the League of Nations without armed force, though what would be done when one of the members of the League of Nations broke away was not clear at the time. The League of

Nations was a promise for the future. It was not dealt with at Paris at all.

The Peace Conference at Paris spent more time drawing up frontiers in central and eastern Europe than in dealing with the German frontiers which were done in a couple of days. The whole of east Europe was in a turmoil. The older states, particularly Austria-Hungary, had collapsed and great stretches of territory were disputed. Broadly speaking, the various committees drawn up tended, when they were faced with a decision to make between two powers, always to support the allied power, or one which had claimed to be the allied power. This is very true in regard to Italy. Italy had been promised South Tyrol. South Tyrol was inhabited by Germans. But because Italy had won, German-speaking Austria was given to Italy. More gravely than this, in what you might call the

The 'white terror' in Hungary: after the destruction of Béla Kun's Republic of Councils, Horthy's counter-revolutionaries rampaged through the country. Here they pose with one of their victims

eastern side of Italy the territory which had been Austrian was inhabited by Yugoslavs, partly by Croats, mainly by Slovenes. But the Italians said, 'We can't allow them to go into the hands of Slovenes or Croats because that would give us an enemy on our frontier.' And a great block, most of the Slovenes of Austria, were in fact transferred to Italy and were not liberated from Italy after the second world war.

Hungary, as I have said, came off very badly. Whenever there was a decision to be made as to how the territories should go, it went against the Hungarians. The Hungarians lost a great deal of territory to the Czechs, they lost territory to the Rumanians, territory which incidentally is still in Rumanian hands. There is a curious point arising from this too. The Czechs inhabited a territory which had been entirely Austrian — or rather part of the Austrian empire — and if the Austrian empire had been an enemy, then the decision ought to have gone against the Czechs. But the Czechs managed to claim that they had liberated themselves and set up a territory of Czechoslavakia on their own, so the decisions always came down on their side. As a result, out of ten million inhabitants in Czechoslavakia, at least three million were German; and it was this grievance which led Hitler to move against Czechoslovakia twenty years later. It is difficult to believe that it was a grievance without any justification.

The treatment of the Hungarian minority was and is scandalous. They are not allowed to use their own language, they are compelled to use Rumanian, and they are one of the aggrieved nationalities who have gone on being aggrieved right to the present day. This was the doing of the Peace Conference in 1919. But as soon as one looks at it, one is bound to say to oneself, 'What other policy could they have followed?' When they had to decide what should happen over certain territories, they were bound to incline to those who were, or claimed to be, allies. Curiously enough, the British were very soft on the Czechs, although the Czechs had not done any fighting on the allied side, except when Czech prisoners of war in Asia had turned themselves into a Czech legion and fought against the Bolsheviks. It has to be said that that was always a good recommendation in 1919, to be against the Bolsheviks.

There is a great deal more to be said about the Peace Conference, but the two most important things in settling the pattern of Europe were the various indemnities. Poor, reduced Austria (which was bankrupt) had to pay an indemnity; Hungary had to pay an indemnity, although the only way in which she could do it was to borrow money either from American banks or British banks (in the end it was the British banks who paid). And there was plenty that was left over which was to raise problems in the future. Turkey broke away from the system because the Sultan was overthrown (though the allies continued to recognise him) and a new Turkey started in Asia Minor led by Kemal Ataturk. This nearly caused a war in 1922. But in the end Turkey came off much better than anyone else, because by having broken with the Sultan and turned into a rebel revolutionary state, she had been able to assert herself as a great power or something like it. At any rate, the Turks did not pay any indemnity and nor did they lose any territory; rather the reverse.

The gravest problem at the Peace Conference which the leaders were never able to solve was what to do with Soviet Russia. Soviet Russia had made peace with Germany. Then the moment that the Germans gave in, the Bolshevik government had simply repudiated the treaty of Brest Litovsk, and therewith had not paid any more indemnities to the Germans, or indeed to anyone else. The Bolsheviks simply declared their independence.

The allies held a great deal against the Bolsheviks. Firstly, they had made peace. For this they ought to be punished. Secondly, when the peace came they had repudiated the peace treaty with Germany: they were no longer paying indemnities to anyone, but were trying to build up their own state. Thirdly, of course, they were Bolshevik — which was very undesirable in 1919, and one of the minor activities of the Supreme Council was to conduct a very ineffective war of intervention in which the French and the British, and to a lesser extent the Americans, all joined.

Ataturk inspecting a guard of honour

By 1920 the problem had become acute, not in terms of either direct intervention in European Russia or Asiatic Russia, but because Poland, quite without any justification, had decided to reclaim all the territory which she had possessed in the seventeenth century. Marshal Pilsudski led an army as far as Kiev, which is deep inside Russia, not a single Pole inhabiting it. Much to the dismay of everyone, the Bolsheviks hit back. The Red Army, directed by Trotsky, defeated the Poles and drove them right out of Russia, and then advanced on Warsaw. They were within sight of Warsaw, and if they had got there, would certainly have proclaimed a Bolshevik Poland and then marched on into Germany.

Fortunately for the Poles, the Russian advance was stopped, and they were able to counter-advance in their turn and to acquire not only the territory which had been rectified by the allies, but some which they had claimed themselves. Yet Poland was still in danger in August 1920. The French said they must intervene on the Polish side. Lloyd George spoke on the issue and was threatened with a general strike by the TUC. Fortunately, before he had to make a decision — it was quite clear he never intended to support the Poles, he took a very poor view of them and was much more in favour of the Bolsheviks — the whole affair fizzled out. There was no armed assistance from the allies and they regarded Poland with great irritation for having caused this crisis. But the Polish crisis of 1920 was only one of many crises which would originate from the logical consequences of the Peace Treaty of 1919. And in the end it was Poland, which had nearly caused a war in 1920, which caused a war in 1939.

The Russians put out posters saying, 'We're fighting the Polish nobles, not the Polish working people'

77

V

THE SECOND WORLD WAR

CANADA

U. S. S.

U.S.S.R. invaded by Germany 22 June 19
Hostilities cease officially 9 May 1945

U. S. A.

U.S.A. and Britain declare war on Japan 8 December 1941
Capitulation of Japan 2 September 1945

1 **Germany** invades **Poland** 1 September 1939
Poland defeated 28 September 1939
Germany capitulates to the Allies 8 May 1945

2 **Britain** declares war on Germany 3 September 1939
Hostilities in Europe cease 8 May 1945

ATLANTIC OCEAN

SOUTH

AFRICA

AMERICA

*Countries within the British Empire involved in the war
from 3 September 1939 to 8 May 1945*

The Second World War:
Dates when countries engaged and withdrew from hostilities

A N

Japan, already at war with **China** since 1937, attacks Pearl Harbor 7 December 1941
In a state of war with Britain and the U.S.A. from 8 December 1941
Hostilities cease on 2 September 1945

PACIFIC OCEAN

CHINA

INDIA

INDIAN OCEAN

AUSTRALIA

NEW

ZEALAND

3 **France** declares war on Germany 3 September 1939.
Officially, hostilities cease with the
collapse and the armistice of 22 June 1940.
Drawn into last phase in Europe with the
liberation of Paris by General de Gaulle
and the landings in southern France 1944.
Hostilities cease 8 May 1945

4 **Belgium/Netherlands** invaded by Germany 10 May 1940
Capitulation of the Netherlands (15 May), Belgium (28 May)

5 Germany invades **Norway** 9 April 1940
Hostilities cease   10 June 1940

6 **Finland** attacked by U.S.S.R. 30 November 1939
Hostilities cease 12 March 1940 (The Peace of Moscow)
On 29 June 1941 Finland joins attack with
Germany on U.S.S.R. but withdraws by 6 December 1941

7 **Italy** declares war on Britain and France 10 June 1940
Withdrew from the war July 1943

8 **Yugoslavia** invaded 6 April 1941
Capitulated 17 April 1941

9 **Greece** invaded by Italy 28 October 1940,
by Germany 6 April 1941
Final resistance in Crete ended 1 June 1941

The First World War ended with peace, and apart from the Treaty of Brest Litovsk the fighting all came to an end in November 1918.

The Second World War was much more ragged. It began to end as early as June 1940 and it went on, in Japan, until September 1945. In June 1940 France went out of the war and made an armistice with Germany. From 1940 to 1944, official France at any rate was not at war. It is true that parts of France were occupied by the Germans but an unassuming, non-political Frenchman could have passed the years 1940 to 1944 without noticing that there was a war on at all. It was only with the return of De Gaulle and the victory of the allies that France was drawn into the war for the last peace. But there was an actual ending of the war, too, for what was after all a very considerable country. More significant, or more preparatory shall I say, to the ending of the war was the way in which Italy, after some difficulty, drew out of the war in 1943. In July of 1943 Mussolini was overthrown when the official

June 22nd 1940: in the same railway coach and on the same spot in the forest of Compiègne, Hitler made the French sign an armistice just as the Germans had had to in 1918

Mussolini touring Turin Airport in 1939

state council turned against him. He was at first interned and later withdrew into northern Italy to set up the Italian Socialist Republic which did not amount to very much. There was however a new government in Italy officially appointed by the King under Marshal Badoglio and from the beginning, that is to say the end of July 1943, it began to put out feelers for a peace arrangement or armistice or short-lived peace treaty. Negotiations went on until October. Earlier in the year, in January, when President Roosevelt met Churchill in Morocco, he had brought into being a new concept, that of unconditional surrender. Roosevelt said, 'We don't want a lot of negotiations,

Italy declares war on Germany: on October 13th 1943 Marshal Badoglio, Prime Minister after Mussolini's fall, read the declaration

we don't want armistice terms and so on, what we demand from the axis powers is unconditional surrender and we'll accept nothing less.'

The first time that this was discussed with the Italians, it went on for some six weeks, mainly with the British High Command in North Africa. The British High Command simply could not stomach the idea that there should be unconditional surrender and that the allied commanders should be in supreme control of Italy. They negotiated the terms of unconditional surrender so that one can say that, in a sense, Italy made a

85

conditional surrender. It was only when the Italians had accepted the short-term conditions of this very long negotiation that they eventually accepted the longer-term conditions in the course of the autumn. But, there were terms of a sort and, most importantly, Italy — official Italy that is — withdrew from the war and the Italian government put itself under the control of the supreme allied command — at that time headed by a British general.

This was less successful than the British and Americans had hoped for. They believed that when they took over Italy they would be able to put themselves into the position of the Italian government and exercise over Italy the supreme control which previously had belonged to the Italian government itself. They allowed the negotiations to go on too long. By the time that they had agreed on unconditional surrender with Italy, the

President Roosevelt and Winston Churchill in North Africa addressing an audience of war correspondents

Italian partisans in Piedmont conducting a sweep across country

Germans had been able to bring up the German forces to supersede the Italian forces which were now not fighting at all, and to occupy practically the whole of Italy. It was not until mid-1944 that the British and Americans reached Rome and it was not until the very end of the war at the beginning of 1945 that the British and American forces penetrated up into northern Italy. There were two Italies — in fact there were three Italies. There was an Italy exclusively occupied by the allies, there was an Italy exclusively occupied by the Germans and then there was an area in between which was technically under the control of Mussolini and the Italian Socialist Republic. That did not amount to much: he simply had to do what the Germans told him. But Italy, at any rate, became an unusual sort of combatant. The only Italians who did any fighting were not the official Italian army which simply disarmed itself, but the Italian partisans who increased in activity during the last year of the war. This was the most significant withdrawal from the war as a sign that the axis defeat was beginning.

The withdrawal of France in 1940 was a recognition of German power. The withdrawal of Italy from the war in 1943 was significantly enough an indication that Italy, the second axis power, had lost all faith in German victory and was trying to get out of the war. What it meant instead was that the Germans superseded Italian forces and had to exercise military operations in a wider field. It was not until the next year that

Cheering crowds greet the Allies as they finally enter Rome in June 1944

The D-Day Landings

the habit of unconditional surrenders spread. There was
nothing very decisive. What characterised that year was that
it was the great year of fighting. In 1944, indeed, the allied
landings in France after D-Day meant that within a relatively
short time France could be brought into the war and well
before the end of the war the French army was in effective
action. By early 1945 some of the German generals had come
to recognise that the war was lost and that the wisest course
was to make an agreement of some sort with the allies as soon
as possible. The sooner the better, because they might be
allowed to retain some of their authority.

In the late winter — February of 1945 — the German High
Command had a series of unofficial secret negotiations through

Switzerland with the allied High Command. They ran up against the difficulty all the time that the allied High Command had to insist on unconditional surrender whereas what these generals wanted was, of course, conditional surrender in which they would be perhaps even accepted as allies.

There was another difficulty which sprang up for the first time now. Throughout the war Russia, of course, had had to follow an independent path because she was cut off from her allies by the whole of central Europe. As the Russians drew closer into Europe they began to concern themselves that they, as one of the three great powers, should also have a say in dealings with Italy in the west. And when they heard rumours that the secret negotiations from the Germans in Italy were afoot, they accused the western powers of secretly negotiating with the Germans and trying to make a separate peace and

Snipers disrupted General de Gaulle's arrival at Notre-Dame for the triumphal service of Thanksgiving. The crowds, though not de Gaulle, dived for cover

Allied nationals — French, Belgians, Dutch, Poles — making the hazardous crossing of the River Elbe to escape the Soviet advance and reach American lines

then prepare to resist any further Russian advance. These Russian suspicions, which were almost entirely unjustified, made it impossible for the British to go on negotiating with the Germans for fear that the Russians would hear about it and object. Whether the Russians ever negotiated separately with the Germans and tried to deal with them is still a disputed point. It has been alleged that at some time in 1943 Molotov, the then Russian Foreign Minister, flew over to Germany and met Ribbentrop for discussions which went on for two days. This has always been denied by the Russians and it is difficult to substantiate, but at any rate the possibility was there. And one can say on the other side that much earlier in the war there had possibly been some sort of negotiations with the Germans. When Hess came to Britain in 1941 there is every indication that he thought he was going to meet groups of British people who were anxious to sit down and talk about peace with Germany. He never had his conversations, even if they were allowed. In any case that was a long time in the past. By the spring of 1945 the western and the eastern allies were contemplating the certainty that negotiations with the Germans would take place. What actually happened was more complicated.

In the earlier months of 1945, not only the German command in Italy but the German command in western Europe began to urge that there should be some attempts at approaching the allies, particularly the western allies, in order probably by now to make unconditional surrender, but in any case an agreement. What was in the minds of some western commanders already was that if they could make a quick peace with Germany, then the German forces could remain mobilised and could check any Russian attempt to move further into Europe. This again is a dark subject. That there were negotiations with the German army in Italy is certain. Whether there were ever German negotiations with the allies in northern Europe is much more doubtful, for a very simple reason — that right until the last moment Hitler continued to exercise effective supreme control. German generals talked about unconditional surrender, about negotiations with the allies, but they ran up against Hitler's ruthless will. Nobody dared go against him. There was more than one attempt, but none of them came off. And right up until the last minute, in the beginning of May 1945, Hitler was still rigidly determined that resistance should go on to the last German.

It was only the suicide of Hitler at the end of April 1945 that opened the way for the Germans to negotiate with the allies. And the Germans had left it rather late. If they had offered negotiations during the Normandy campaign of 1944, they might have got some response. By 1945 the allies were clearly not only winning, but they were achieving complete success and no longer needed to think of how to eliminate the German

Hitler inspects the damage to his headquarters after the abortive plot to blow him up in July 1944. The Nazis took savage reprisals: some 150 alleged conspirators were executed

armies. The German armies were being defeated, the Russians were on their way to Berlin, and the allies were on their way to the Elbe line. There is no evidence at all that the western powers contemplated doing a deal with the Germans as late as May 1945. As soon as Hitler was dead the remaining authorities in Germany, both the generals and the successor to Hitler, so far as there was one — Hitler claimed to have appointed Admiral Dönitz his successor as Chancellor of Germany, and though Dönitz was shut away somewhere near the frontier of Denmark, insofar as there was a German government after Hitler's death, it was Dönitz's — sent Jodl, one of the Chiefs of Staff, to Paris to offer unconditional surrender.

The deal was done in a very short time, and the surrender marked for most people in the west the end of the war. Or, insofar as we contemplate the war at all now, we think of it as ending on 8th May, for 8th May was the day on which Jodl signed the agreement of unconditional surrender with Eisenhower as Supreme Commander on the western front. The German Marshal Keitel then had to go to Moscow as well or to the Russian front in order to sign the agreement for unconditional surrender to the Russians with Zhukov, and that was not signed until a day later. This explains the curious fact that whereas the western powers celebrate the end of the war on 8th May, the Russians and the rest of the eastern front

The unconditional surrender of the German army being signed by Colonel-General Gustaf Jodl, Chief of Staff

celebrate the end of the war on 9th May, the day after.

The war in Europe was ended. There were confused times. For instance, by June 1945 British troops in northern Italy were contemplating having to go to war with Yugoslavia, an ally, who had insisted on occupying more than (or what the British said was more than) her share. The Yugoslavs occupied some stretches of Trieste but never managed to occupy it all and in time were persuaded to go away again. For all practical purposes the European war stopped.

The war had stopped on the western front, it had stopped on the eastern front, it had stopped in the Balkans. One war was still in full spate, and that was the Japanese war. Until this time the Japanese war had been very much an American affair. The Americans had conducted the whole show and were gradually driving the Japanese back into a position of defeat. But the Japanese, although they recognised that they were going to lose the war, were determined not to surrender, or not to offer unconditional surrender. What is more, there was — and this had been a characteristic of Japanese policy all along — more than one group. There were sensible, moderate statesmen who had never liked the war against the allies and would have been glad to get out of the war on moderate terms as early as possible. There was a hard militarist group, who had dominated Japanese policy ever since 1931, who thought in terms of military control and advance and had, of course, carried Japanese authority far down into the Pacific Ocean. The Japanese were now in retreat, but it was a retreat which had only just begun and the militarist group were prepared to argue. They argued two things: that the longer the war went on, the more likely it was that Japan could get more tolerable terms; and, simply, that Japan ought not to offer any terms at any time but compel the allies to destroy Japan literally before they would agree to ending of the war.

By 1945 the balance was shifting somewhat from the out-and-out militarists to those who were prepared to negotiate. In June and early July the Japanese government made approaches through Russia, offering a peace of unconditional surrender on honourable terms to the Americans. The offer never reached

US Marines rush to be part of an heroic picture as they raise the
Stars and Stripes on Iwo Jima in February 1945 for the camera.
The island became a vital advance base for American bombers
targeted on Japan

the Americans, because Stalin, once the European war was over, was anxious that Russia should enter the Far Eastern war and acquire territory which the Russians had previously lost, after the war of 1905 and at other times. Unfortunately he had no troops in the Far East and this would take him some time. Therefore it was essential to Stalin that the war should go on, so that then he could move in and perhaps even occupy parts of Japan before the Americans were there at all.

This threw out all the Japanese calculations. They had assumed that they could use Russia, they had used Russia for a long time as a negotiating agent and had been conciliatory towards Russia, and the Russians had been conciliatory towards Japan until the war ended. But once the war ended then Russia could turn around and simply prepare for a new war against Japan.

The Japanese could not bring themselves to make any direct offer until the last minute to the American government, and the American government was now in a great quandary. How should they complete the defeat of Japan? The navy said that they should rely on the blockade and that this would bring Japan to surrender. The army said that the American army should land in Japan and, despite the fact that there would then be enormous casualties, should go on to occupy Japan. The army preparations were not even made. It meant that the war would drift on for a long time to come. The navy argument did not demand so many casualties, but it too demanded time. Early in August came the first indications that Japan was prepared to offer unconditional surrender. The one condition that the Japanese made was that they should retain their Emperor. And this, at first, was the one condition which the Americans would not accept because, quite wrongly, they blamed the Emperor for the war. The Emperor had been opposed to the war before it started and during it, but despite his so-called standing he had no real power: he had to do what the generals said.

The Americans were gloomily contemplating a war that seemed to be going on for ever when there arose ready, prepared, the atom bomb. The scientists insisted they must

The cloud over Hiroshima. American scientists had argued that the atom bomb had to be used to justify its expense to the US Congress

use it in order to justify to Congress all the money that had been spent on it. They had no idea what it would be like, they had no idea of the extent of the destruction; but there was dropped first a bomb on Hiroshima and then a bomb on Nagasaki. Both of them caused terrible destruction and ghastly sufferings to the Japanese people. The first one left the Japanese dazed. The second led the Emperor to resolve, against the generals' will, against the risk to his own life from the extremists, that, as he said, 'The war must come to an end. We must endure the unendurable.' And on 17th August he announced over the radio that he personally was accepting unconditional surrender. This was, to all practical purposes, the end of the war. Technically, however, it was not the end of the war. This is a quaint little feature to the end of the story.

The unconditional surrender had to be made to a superior high-standing American authority. There was only one American authority of the first rank in the vicinity: the Supreme Commander, General MacArthur. But General MacArthur was in the Philippines and it took him ten days to come up on a battleship to Tokyo Harbour. There, on 2nd September, a Japanese statesman signed the agreement of unconditional surrender, and with that General MacArthur became, for the next five years almost, supreme ruler of Japan. The Second World War was over.

*One of the last great moments of the battleship in modern
warfare: the signing of Japan's unconditional surrender*

VI

PRESENT CHAOS

There is a curious thing about the earlier great wars which I have been talking about. Each ended with a great conference. The War of 1814 ended with the Congress of Vienna. The First World War of the twentieth century ended with the Paris Peace Conference in the first six months of 1919.

The greatest of all wars so far, the Second World War, ended raggedly. People find it very difficult to define the moment and say, 'Now the Second World War is over.' Normally what we do is accept the day of 8th May 1945, when the Germans agreed to unconditional surrender. But that only affected one war, the war against Germany. If we were talking about the Italian war we would say either in 1943, when some of Italy agreed to unconditional surrender or, more technically, 1947 when the Allies negotiated a peace treaty. But if we were to say that we should wait till the last peace treaty, the final one which finished all wars, that would be the Allied Treaty with Japan in 1951. Then again, this is difficult because Russia made a different treaty with Japan after objecting to the proposals that our allies were making. And if we are to say that war ended when a state of peace was declared with Germany, then that could be either 1955 or even 1958. In 1955 the western powers, Great Britain and the United States, recognised what we came to call the Federal State of Germany, that is to say western Germany, as a sovereign state no longer under Allied occupation. It would be possible to wait until the Russians recognised the East German state as a separate body. That would be either earlier or later.

It also becomes rather hard to get people to agree *where* the war ended. I think I am right in saying that the war has ended now. But it took at least ten years to get it tidied up.

What were the great obstacles and where were the stages of the ending of the war? In one sense, as I say, there was a dramatic ending of what was the biggest war, that is to say the war against the allies, Great Britain, Russia, the United States, which ended with the unconditional surrender of Germany on either 8th May or, according to Russian calculations, 9th May. But there was no agreement of peace for a very long time.

103

*Where German postwar reconstruction started. This photograph
was taken in Berlin*

In 1945, at the surrender, the greatest dispute between the
allies was the question of reparations. The Americans, being
very rich, said they did not want any reparations and that
therefore nor should the allies have reparations either. The
Russians said their whole country had been devastated by the
Germans and the Germans must pay a great deal. Grudgingly,
the Americans agreed to this in principle, but when it came to
the practical application of it, they objected because they said,
'What is happening is that we are paying the Germans to get
Germany on its feet and you're taking away from Germany

The Potsdam Conference, attended by Stalin, Truman, Churchill and Attlee to settle the occupation of Germany

what we're giving.' But it was not until at least five years after 1945 that the Russians stopped demanding, and not always getting, reparations. Then again, the other great dispute among the allies — the victors — in 1945 was not about Germany at all, it was about Poland.

This is a fascinating thing. The great dispute in 1814 between the allies was about Poland. One of the great disputes among the allies, England and France, in 1919 and particularly in 1920 was over Poland. The most practical dispute which ran on throughout the meeting of the allies at Potsdam in 1945 was about Poland, or rather about Poland's western frontier.

In 1920 Poland conquered a lot of what had previously been

Russian territory. The Russians had always resented this. When they became the victors, they drove through this territory and took it back from Poland. Poland was thus deprived of territory. People said, 'We can't have that because Poland was numbered among the victors. It's particularly hard to take any territory from her because she has been so appallingly treated by Germany and has been such a gallant resister.' So the Poles were compensated by being given a great stretch of German territory, the frontier as it is now called of the Oder and the Neisse Line. This territory was not inhabited by Poles. And it seemed impossible for the Poles to take territory inhabited by Germans. There was, however, a simple solution which could be applied because a state of war existed. A great deal of the territory which Poland acquired had already been evacuated by its German inhabitants out of terror — although in the course of 1945 and 1946 seven million more Germans were driven out of their homes into western Germany. They have never gone back, and the territory has instead been inhabited by Poles mainly from the territory which Russia had taken from Poland. Now a whole generation has passed and people are beginning to forget these now old frontiers — or I wonder if they are?

This was not the only expulsion of populations that went on in 1945. Something like three million Germans were expelled from Czechoslovakia. People who had been in that territory as long as the Czechs themselves — maybe a thousand years — out they went in 1945. And these were not the only people who were expelled from Czechoslovakia. About 300,000 Hungarians (or to be correct, Slovaks who had been originally Hungarians) were cleared out. There were other minorities who were perhaps in the worst situation of all. Rumania and Hungary had both, very unwillingly, fought on the German side. Rumania had been able to jump about three months, perhaps six months, before the end of the war and be counted as an ally. Hungary,

German refugees pouring over the new border into West Germany in November 1945

The frontiers of Central European countries after the
Peace Treaties following the end of the Second World War

NORTH SEA

UNITED
KINGDOM

London

NETHERLANDS

WEST

EAST
Berlin
Potsdam
GERMANY

Elbe

Oder
Neisse

BELGIUM

GERMANY
Bonn

Leipzig

Dresden

Prague

C Z E C

Seine

Paris

Saarland
(to Germany 1957)

Strasbourg

Danube

Vie

FRANCE

Rhine

Bern
SWITZ.

AUSTRI

Trieste

Rijeka

A
D
R
I
A
T
I
C

SPAIN

Corsica

I
T
A
L
Y

Rome

Sardinia

MEDITERRANEAN SEA

Sicily

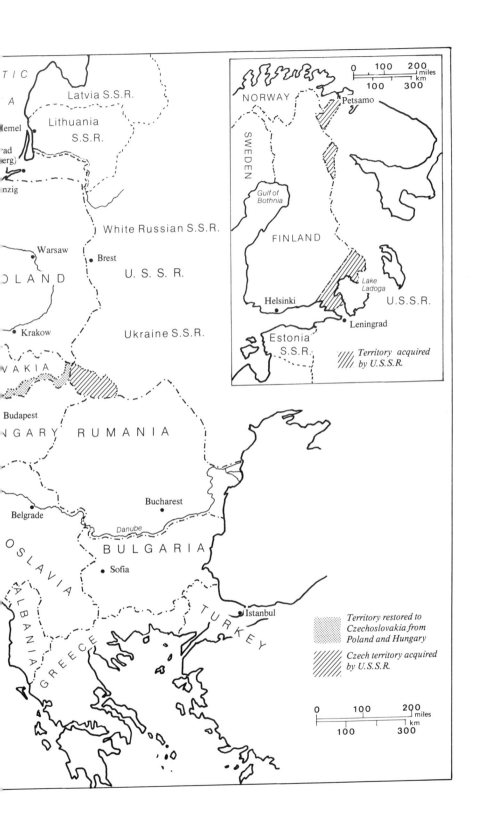

TIC

A

Latvia S.S.R.

Lithuania
S.S.R.

emel

ad
erg)

nzig

White Russian S.S.R.

Warsaw

Brest

OLAND

U. S. S. R.

Krakow

Ukraine S.S.R.

VAKIA

Budapest

NGARY RUMANIA

Belgrade

Bucharest

Danube

OSLAVIA

BULGARIA

Sofia

ALBANIA

GREECE

TURKEY

Istanbul

NORWAY

Petsamo

SWEDEN

Gulf of
Bothnia

FINLAND

Lake
Ladoga

Helsinki

Leningrad

U.S.S.R.

Estonia
S.S.R.

Territory acquired
by U.S.S.R.

0   100   200
               miles
     100   300
               km

Territory restored to
Czechoslovakia from
Poland and Hungary

Czech territory acquired
by U.S.S.R.

0   100   200
                     miles
         100   300
                     km

owing to the fumbling nature of the Horthy government, tried to get out of the war and failed. Therefore Rumania was treated as an ally whereas Hungary was treated as an enemy. Rumania as a result was given some territory in Transylvania. Half a million Hungarians lived there, and live there now, treated very badly because they are not given their national rights. All in all, it was an even worse sorting-out than had been attempted in 1918 and 1919.

This was one of the negotiations. But there were far more difficult problems. The Conference of Potsdam in July 1945 was the last of the great gatherings, though not great in terms of number of assembly. Potsdam was simply the last meeting of the so-called great powers: the United States, Soviet Russia, Great Britain. Later, though some of their representatives met again, the heads of state never met in grandeur as they had done in Teheran, in Yalta and in Potsdam. And the Potsdam Conference, far from leading to any conclusion, led to estrangement. One very significant thing was that when President Truman went to Potsdam it was the first time he had ever been out of the United States. This in itself marked a very great change. One distinguishing feature of President Roosevelt was that he, in his skilful way, had wanted to be on good terms with Russia and had managed to be at the Teheran conference and at the Yalta conference. Indeed, one could go further and say that Yalta was the only meeting of the three great powers and therefore the only meeting of the great world powers in history which was a success, where all three wanted to work together and reach agreements.

Already at Potsdam Russia and the United States wanted to encourage conflict and to win against each other. There has never been, from that day to this, a really satisfactory meeting of the great powers; of their more modest representatives perhaps, but never of the great rulers again. When Truman came to Potsdam, he had with him a piece of secret knowledge. He believed that the first nuclear weapon would be used in the course of the summer, but until it was used he could not be sure it would succeed. It had never been tried out. When Truman was on the way back to America, he got the news on board ship that the nuclear bomb had been dropped over Hiroshima and he exclaimed, 'This is a great day in the history of the world!' He had no idea how great it was going to be and what troubles it was going to cause.

Why was the nuclear weapon used over Japan? Japan was seeking to make peace. She had sent her messages through Russia, which the Russian government had not passed on because they did not want to — they wanted to get their blow of war in. The American army and the American navy both offered eventual solutions, but there was something more than this. The scientists and technical advisers who had developed the nuclear bomb insisted that if it were to be tried, it must be tried on a real target, so that Congress should be satisfied with all the money that it had paid. Therefore the first bomb was dropped on Hiroshima not to lead to the collapse of Japan, or even to lead to peace offers from Japan, because Japan was only too eager now to make peace offers. It was dropped as a demonstration to the American Congress.

Nobody knew what it was going to be like. Nobody had conceived the terrible devastation that was caused. What is more, the Japanese did not immediately respond by unconditional surrender. Indeed they tended to take the view, 'Well that's a bomb. We've lost 50,000 people and more killed at Hiroshima, but now the situation is as before.' The Americans had two bombs: one they could use at Hiroshima, and had done; the second, they said they must use, otherwise the Japanese would think that the Hiroshima bomb was the only one, whereas if they used two the Japanese would be overwhelmed. Even though the Japanese might have said after the dropping of the bomb on Nagasaki, 'All right, that's it. We'll stand these two catastrophes and continue with the war.' As it was — this is a very dramatic episode in history — the Japanese government ministers were fully clear that there must be unconditional surrender. None of them dared do it because they said, 'If any of us takes the lead and offers unconditional surrender to the Americans, we shall be massacred by nationalistic Japanese fanatics.' The Emperor who had never given a lead in policy in his life, or one might say also in history — the Emperor was a figurehead — asserted himself for the first and last time. In the late days of August 1945 he went on the air and announced unconditional surrender. But, as I said earlier, it was not until 1951 that the peace treaty with Japan was signed, simply because the Russians put forward terms to which the allies would not agree and eventually Japan had to make a separate treaty with Russia.

Meanwhile, the other treaties went forward, and there are great curiosities there. Italy had been, for something like three years, an enemy. One Italian government, though not a government which exercised authority over all Italy, not at any rate until the last days in 1945, had come over and was accepted somewhat grudgingly as an ally, or at any rate as a co-operator with the allied forces. The other one technically remained an enemy although it did not do anything as an

Japanese officers surrendering their swords in Malaya

enemy. When, in 1947, a peace conference was held in Paris, Italy was the first country that the allies dealt with. There were two territorial topics which concerned the allies. One was whether any of South Tyrol should be restored to Austria, bearing in mind that it was inhabited by Germans or German-speaking people. It was easy enough for the allies to decide this, since they could say, 'No, Italy should have it, because she's been an ally for a short time and the Austrians were never allies.' Much trickier was the fact that the Yugoslavs, who had been our allies throughout the war, were laying claim to Trieste. But now the Yugoslavs were taking a Communist line of their own, and as Communists they could not be given Trieste; it had to go to the former enemy, Italy, and that was the arrangement of the treaty which was finally made in 1947. There remained plenty of other treaties to make. Rumania and Bulgaria made peace fairly quickly and there was nothing much one could dispute, except Transylvania. Hungary was accepted.

Austria was a difficult case. It was like Germany, or rather it had been part of greater Germany but had managed to jump aside in time, and before the end of the war it had again become independent under Chancellor Renner (who had also made Austria an independent republic at the end of the First War in 1918). Austria was now a small independent republic. Who should garrison it? The four powers agreed that it should pass under their combined authority. Each had a zone of occupation, all four of them occupied Vienna. It was the only place where full allied co-operation continued for ten years after the war. To have a picture of Vienna under allied occupation, remember the Orson Welles film *The Third Man*. The other remarkable thing about Austria is that the allies actually agreed in the end that she should be a neutral state. She was not allowed to join any of the alliances; she could have her own army and so on, but she was to remain totally independent of the coalitions. She was not an associate of the British and Americans, she was not an associate of the French, she was not an associate of the Russians. She was a guaranteed

EROI (!) sotto LISA 1866
EROI (!) sotto ADUA
EROI (!) DI KAPORETTO
EROI (!) in ALBANIA 1940
EROI (!) in JUGOSLAVIA 1941-45
EROI (!) in... 1952

F.N.R.J.

*A Yugoslav banner pokes fun at Italy's military defeats in a
demonstration protesting at the return of Trieste to the Italians*

An international police patrol in Vienna

neutral independent state, which you might think set an example to a number of the other small independent states. It certainly worked in the case of Austria.

But the biggest problem, one which almost goes on to the present day — something of it is certainly still with us — was Germany. It was not for some years that the American Congress resolved that a state of war with Germany had ceased to exist. It was not until 1955 that the Americans actually recognised that Federal Germany should have its own independence. Eastern Germany was under Russian occupation and has remained to this day a separate state, completely under Russian control and accepting Russian direction more

150,000 West Berliners celebrate the end of the ten-month blockade

The Berlin Wall began — demolishing homes, separating families — and was reinforced until only slits were left, manned constantly by East German soldiers with machine guns

than the independent Communist states such as Czechoslovakia and Hungary and Rumania do. These were not the only problems that came up. In the centre of the two conflicting states there was Berlin, which was divided into four, three of them belonging to the three parts of Germany belonging to the western powers, one part under Russian control. And Berlin has become not gradually more united but more divided. Berlin was divided in 1960 at the great wall which still exists there. There was an alarm in 1948 when the Russians stopped land transport, road transport and rail transport, from western Germany into Berlin, to which the allies replied, to everyone's astonishment, successfully with an air lift, which went on for something like a year. The American and British air forces carried everything into western Berlin. Western Germany maintained its independence or separation from Russian control and has retained it.

However, Europe still bears the scars of the Second World War and now seems as if it is resigned to them. There are still millions of Germans who complain at being evacuated from their home all those, nearly 40 years ago. There are hundreds of thousands of Hungarians who grieve at being expelled from their homes in Czechoslovakia. One could go on reciting the various things that have happened. But the greatest legacy we have had from World War Two is without a doubt the development of nuclear fission, and the transformation of this into nuclear weapons. This has now become the most terrifying, the greatest and most threatening danger that hangs over civilisation.

However, do not worry. The Third World War will be the last.

The shape of the Cruise missile. American B52G bombers have been equipped to carry twelve each

INDEX

Rome, allied entry into (1944), 87, 88
Roosevelt, President Franklin D., 86, 110; and unconditional surrender, 84-5; and Soviet Russia, 110
Rumania, 64, 73, 106, 113, 117; obtains territory in Transylvania, 110
Russia, 27; and Napoleon, 5-8, 10, 12-14; Congress of Vienna, 23; and Poland, 25; Crimean War, 34-5; and First World War, 42; revolution (March 1917), 44; Bolshevik Revolution (November 1917), 44 *See also* Soviet Russia
Russo-Turkish War (1877), 36, 61

St. Germain, Treaty of, 61
Salisbury, Lord, 36
Scapa Flow, 69
Sebastopol, defence of, 36
Slovenes of Austria, transferred to Italy, 73
Smuts, General Jan Christiaan, 44, 71
South Tyrol, 72, 113
Soviet Russia: allied intervention (1919-21), 53, 74-6; war with Poland (1920), 75-7; Second World War: advance into Germany, 90-1; and Japan, 97, 103; reparations, 104-5; and Poland, 106; and USA, 110; and East Germany, 115

Spain: and Napoleon, 5; Congress of Vienna, 23; liberal movement and civil war, 32-4
Stalin, Josef, 45, 105; and Japan, 97
Stockholm Conference (1917), 42
Supreme War Council (1918), 63

Talleyrand, 16, 23, 25, 27
Teheran Conference (1943), 110
Third Man, The, film, 113
Transylvania, 110, 113
Trianon, Treaty of the, 61
Trieste, 95, 113, 114
Trotsky, Leon, 45-6, 76
Truman, President Harry S., 105, 110-11
Turkey, 34, 35; war with Russia (1877), 36, 61; First World War, 49; armistice, 50; and the peace treaty, 61, 74; and Kemal Ataturk, 74

Unconditional surrender, concept of, 84-6, 89, 90, 92, 94, 99-100
United States: First World War, 41; entry into war, 41; war aims, 41; and the armistice, 52; Paris Peace Conference, 67; and Japan in Second World War, 95-100; choices for defeat of Japan, 97; and the atom bomb, 97-9; and Soviet Russia, 110

Venice, 17-18; loss of its
  independence, 24, 26
Venizelos, Eleutherios, 71
Verona, Congress of, 33
Versailles, Settlement or
  Treaty of, 61, 67, 69
  See also Paris Peace
  Conference
Vesnitch, M., 71
Vienna, 113, 115; Congress of,
  23-30, 34, 35, 103

War criminals (1919), 68
Waterloo, battle of, 17
Welles, Orson, 113
Wellington, Duke of, 33
Wemyss, Admiral, 52

West Germany, 103, 115, 117;
  Polish refugees in, 106-7
Western Alliance, 33
Wilhelm II, Kaiser, 49; takes
  refuge in Netherlands, 68
Wilson, President Woodrow,
  48-9; and war aims, 41; his
  Fourteen Points, 49, 64-5;
  and the armistice, 49; at
  Paris Peace Conference, 62,
  63; and the League of
  Nations, 70, 71

Yalta Conference (1945), 110
Yugoslavia, 50, 63, 95, 113, 114

Zhukov, Marshal, 94